When Catherine the Great and I Were Eight!

by Cari Best pictures by Giselle Potter

Melanie Kroupa Books   FARRAR, STRAUS AND GIROUX · NEW YORK

For Uncle Bob
and John Philip Sousa—
you made the car dance
—C.B.

For Olive
—G.P.

PRONUNCIATION GUIDE

Nyet! means *No!*

Say: Knee-yet (together fast)

Da! means *Yes!*

Say: Dot (without the "t")

Text copyright © 2003 by Cari Best
Illustrations copyright © 2003 by Giselle Potter
All rights reserved
Distributed in Canada by Douglas & McIntyre Ltd.
Color separations by Hong Kong Scanner Arts
Printed and bound in the United States of America by Berryville Graphics
Designed by Nancy Goldenberg
First edition, 2003
1 3 5 7 9 10 8 6 4 2

Library of Congress Cataloging-in-Publication Data
Best, Cari.
    When Catherine the Great and I were eight! / by Cari Best ; pictures by Giselle Potter.
        p.   cm.
    Summary: Sara, her Russian grandmother, her mother, and some neighbors try to drive
to the beach on a very hot day.
    ISBN 0-374-39954-9
    [1. Grandmothers—Fiction.   2. Automobile travel—Fiction.   3. Heat—Fiction.
4. Neighbors—Fiction.   5. Russian Americans—Fiction.]   I. Potter, Giselle, ill.   II. Title.

PZ7.B46575 Wh 2005
[E]—dc21

                                                                                            2002026504

A long time ago, Catherine the Great, my Russian grandma, lived in a big white house near a big black sea far away from America. When she was eight, she liked to float like a flower in a bathing suit with long sleeves, long stripes, and long stockings. Now I'm eight, and I wish I could float like a flower, too. "You could, Sara," Grandma tells me. "One day I'll show you."

My city in the summer is like an oven that's been baking.

"Mee-owww!" says Mr. Minsky's cat when she lands on our stoop. Nellie, the downstairs dog, is too hot to chase her, and Monica's dad cuts his hair really short.

Mama and I watch Grandma fold her Russian newspaper into a fan, and Monica, my friend, waters her feet instead of the flowers.

"I like the beach in June," sings Mary Caruso, and everyone, including her big baby, Mimmo, says, "Yesss!" except for Grandma, who says, "Da!"

Then in go the beach towels, the blankets, and the lunches. In go the straw hats, the lotion, and the toys. In go the beach people . . . "Hurry, Sara!" calls Monica, and Mr. Minsky's old car chugs away.

But not very far away because Grandma says, "Wait! I forgot my bathing suit."
So back we go to get it—the one with the accordion skirt.

But not before Mr. Minsky says, "Oh, Catherine!" because he is
not very good at U-turning, and copycat Mimmo says,
"Oh, Catherine!" because he just likes to repeat everything.

Then off we go for the second time: three in the radio seat, three in the sandwich seat, and two in the carsick seat in the way, way back.

"Turn on the air!" we shout. So Mr. Minsky puts down the window. "Ahhh!"

"*Now* is everybody happy?" he asks, and everyone, including copycat Mimmo, says, "Yes!" except for Grandma, who says, "*Da!*"

Then Mary Caruso's favorite song comes on, and she sings while Mr. Minsky makes the old car dance. And everyone feels good to be going someplace cool when it's hotter than a hot potato on this boiling summer day.

Soon we're out of our neighborhood and into someone else's: people walking with sun umbrellas, fire hydrants like Niagara Falls, sprinklers making swaying showers, and little plastic pools waiting for waves and splashes. Monica and I wiggle in our sticky seats, pretending we're the Beach Girls swimming without any water.

But not for long because all of a sudden
Grandma says, "S-T-O-P stop!" which makes Mary
Caruso stop singing and the old car stop dancing and
everyone stop breathing—except for Mama, who asks,
"What's the matter?"

Then Grandma, who is just learning to read English, says, "Nothing is the matter.
I was just reading the sign: S-T-O-P," which makes Mr. Minsky say, "Oh,
Catherine!" and Mimmo say, "Oh, Catherine!" and me say, "Oh no!" because
I'm the one who's been teaching her to read English.

There is traffic in front of us, traffic behind us, and traffic on both sides. "It's bumper to bumper on the highway to the beach," says the lady on the radio.

"Don't we know it!" says Monica's dad. "Don't we know it!" says
Mimmo. "We're hot!" Monica and I shout. And Grandma says,
"Everybody have patience."

But nobody seems to have any because now we're standing so still that the people in the car ahead of us are getting out to stretch. Then *we* get out to stretch. Grandma and Mr. Minsky decide it's a good time for a Russian ballet. Everyone around us claps, and of course Mimmo claps, too.

But not for long because here comes the ice cream man pedaling between the cars. "Ice cream before lunch?" asks Mama. "Why not!" says Grandma, and she buys each of us something cold and sweet.

Then back to the car we go—just in time,
because now the traffic has started to move.
"Yippee!" we shout, running and dripping and
laughing and licking . . . settling ourselves in
for the rest of the ride.

But not for long because Monica says, "I feel sick." And Mimmo says, "I feel sick." And Grandma says, "Sick? I have something to make you feel better." And she gives Monica a piece of lemon to suck on. And one to Mimmo, too.

Then we ride and we ride and Monica's sweaty legs are touching my sweaty legs and neither of us likes it one bit. So Grandma says, "Let's play our game of going places, Last Letter!" And everyone agrees.

Everyone except Mimmo, who is too tired to talk. Here is how we play: "Russia," says Grandma. And since "a" is the last letter in "Russia," Monica's dad thinks of "Amsterdam." "Mmmmm," says Mr. Minsky. "How about Miami!" Then Mary Caruso sings "Italy!" and Mama answers, "Yankee Stadium," which is where she'd be if we weren't going to the beach.

Monica says, "Minnesota," and when it's my turn, I say, "Atlantic Ocean"—the place I want to be right this very minute.

"We're getting there," says Mr. Minsky as the old car dances down the road. But before anyone can say "New York," something happens to end our game.

Rattle, rattle, click, click. Mr. Minsky's car starts to make a funny noise like a fan with a rock stuck inside it. *Rattle, rattle, click, click.*

"Now what?" asks Mary Caruso as Mr. Minsky pulls the car over.

"Now what?" asks Mimmo, who is suddenly wide-awake.

"Oh no!" we all say, wondering if we'll *ever* get to the beach.

"Let's see," says Mr. Minsky, opening the hood and looking around inside. After a long time he says, "Here's the trouble: the little pin that holds everything together has flown the coupe—it's gone!" He draws a picture of it in the air with his finger.

Everyone paces back and forth trying to figure out what to do.

"It's gone," says Mimmo. And we all nod our heads. Monica and I are ready to give up.

Until Grandma says, "Look here!" and she pulls out one of the silver hairpins that are holding up her hair. "You have to use your head," she says.

So Mr. Minsky does. "The car has to cool down before I can try Catherine's hairpin," he says.

So we wait and we sweat and we take turns peeing behind the bushes because it's the only private place around for miles.

And then Mr. Minsky asks, "Isn't this fun?" and we all say, "NO!" except for Grandma, who says, "Da!"

Then finally it's time to try the hairpin! All we can see of Mr. Minsky is the back of his shorts. *Moan, groan, bend, scrape, turn, twist, whistle, squeak*, is what we hear while he works under the hood.

And then what do we hear? *Hum, hum, hummy, hum*, as the car starts up again. "Oh, Catherine!" says Mr. Minsky, rushing over to give her a big kiss. "You *are* the greatest!" Then Mimmo says, "Oh, Catherine! You *are* the greatest!" and Grandma has to hold up her face to get kisses from us all.

Then we pile into the car again and chug-chug-chug away. But not very far away because Monica and I say, "We're starving!" And Mimmo says, "We're starving!" And everyone else says, "It's lunchtime!"

So what do we do? We park our sweaty selves under a big green tree and have our beach picnic before we even get to the beach . . . and wash it all down with the ice-cold lemonade that Grandma made before we left.

"Maybe we should turn around and go home," says Mr. Minsky, looking at his watch. And before anyone can say "Okay," Grandma says, "*Nyet!*" because she knows we're almost there.

The sun is not very high in the six o'clock sky when we finally put our feet on the beach. We have the sand and the water—*and* the mosquitoes—all to ourselves.

Monica and I are the first ones to get wet. Then Nellie, Mr. Minsky, Mama, and Monica's dad. Mary Caruso and Mimmo come right after. "Come in, Grandma," I shout. "The water feels delicious."

First Grandma wets her hands, then her face. Her shoulders are next, and finally her bathing suit—the one with the accordion skirt. As quick as a wink, she's on her back— arms out, shoulders back, head on the water, toes straight up.

"I wish I could float like a flower," I say, trying and sinking and spitting out water with salt.

"You could, Sara," says Grandma, pushing away the water with her big arms. "Let me show you."

Then, before I know it, one big arm is under my back, the other under my legs. "Make your back like a bridge," she says. And at first I think I can't.

But then I can!

Here I am with Catherine the Great, my Russian grandma, both of us in our new bathing suits, floating like flowers . . . on a big blue sea.

"Isn't it easy?" Grandma asks. "Just like when I was eight."

And this time I say, *"Da!"*